P9-BYA-792

The First Day
of
Winter

Consie Powell

Albert Whitman & Company, Morton Grove, Illinois

*For Mom, with loving thanks for
my cold-weather genes.*

*Special thanks to Rog for dreaming up our 1995 Christmas card.
Those festive words were the seeds that grew into this book.*

Library of Congress Cataloging-in-Publication Data

Powell, Consie.
The first day of winter / written and illustrated by Consie Powell.
p. cm.
ISBN 0-8075-2450-6 (hardcover)
1. Natural history–Outdoor books–Juvenile literature. 2. Winter–Juvenile literature.
3. Cold adaptation–Juvenile literature. 4. Outdoor recreation–Juvenile literature. I. Title.
QH81.P856 2005   508.2–dc22   2005002742

Text and illustrations copyright © 2005 by Constance Buffington Powell.
Published in 2005 by Albert Whitman & Company, 6340 Oakton Street, Morton Grove, Illinois, 60053–2723.
Published simultaneously in Canada by Fitzhenry & Whiteside, Markham, Ontario.
Printed in the United States of America.
10 9 8 7 6 5 4 3 2 1

The illustrations are created in ink, watercolor, and colored pencil.
The design is by Consie Powell and Carol Gildar.

For more information about Albert Whitman & Company,
please visit our web site at www.albertwhitman.com.

As autumn passes, days grow short. In the northern part of the country, chilly nights leave a frosty dawn. Soon snow falls, and before long, days and nights are cold enough for snow to stay on the ground. October is over, November is done. Now it's the twenty-first of December, the shortest day of the year. It's the First Day of Winter!

Bundle up – it's time to go outside and have some fun. But don't forget to look around. There's a lot more going on in the woods during winter than meets the eye.

On the first day of winter,
come spend some time with me!
We'll hide and seek beneath the limbs
of one big old fir tree.

EVERGREEN FIR TREE HAS WAXY NEEDLES AND A CONE SHAPE

Look for
one nearby tall tree
that stays green all year.

On the second day of winter,
let's hurry out to play.
With two big tubes for sledding,
we'll zoom and spin – hooray!

RAVEN SLIDES AND ROLLS   OTTER BOUNDS AND SLIDES

Watch for
two playful sliders –
one with fur, one with feathers.

On the third day of winter,
out in the cold we go.
We'll make three merry angels
pressed in the sparkling snow.

OWL CAUGHT A MOUSE   RUFFED GROUSE LEFT A SNOW BURROW   PINE SISKINS FORAGED FOR SEEDS

Find
three sets of marks
in the drifts.

On the fourth day of winter,
the sky's a brilliant blue.
Four hours of lively skating
will warm us through and through.

DRAGONFLY NYMPHS PROWL · SNAPPING TURTLE WAITS IN THE MUD · BEAVER FETCHES A WILLOW BRANCH · BLUEGILLS SLOWLY SWIM

Discover what
four kinds of animals are doing
under the ice.

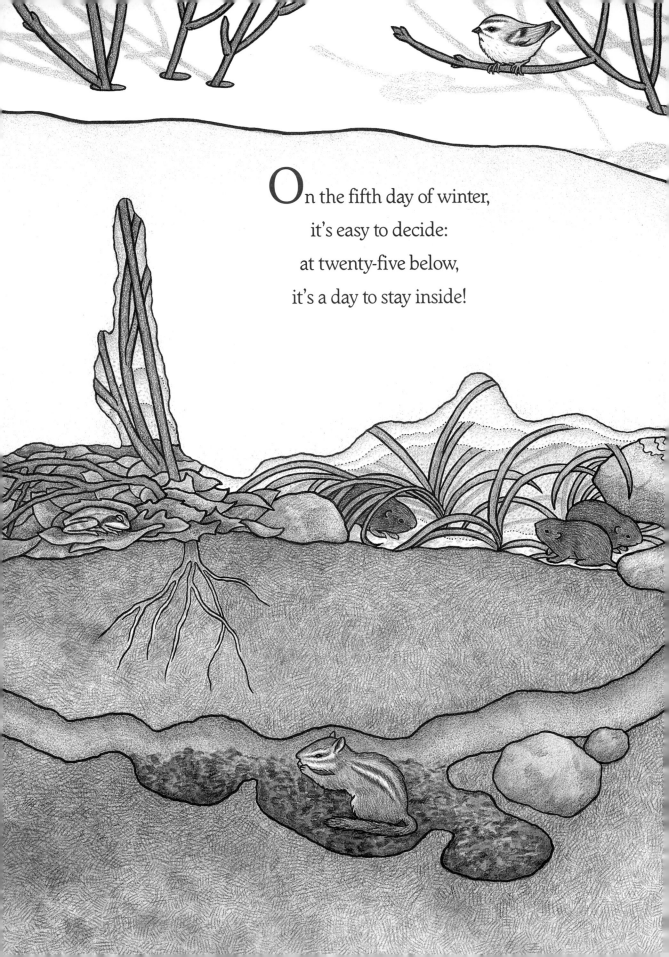

On the fifth day of winter,
it's easy to decide:
at twenty-five below,
it's a day to stay inside!

SLEEPY CHIPMUNK NIBBLES SEEDS · VOLES HUDDLE UNDER THE SNOW · ICY WOOD FROG WAITS FOR SPRING · KINGLETS HUNT FOR FROZEN CATERPILLARS · GARTER SNAKES HIBERNATE

*See how
five types of critters
deal with the cold.*

On the sixth day of winter,
as snowflakes fill the air,
six warm and woolly mittens
are just the thing to wear.

SIX-POINTED STARS · HEXAGONS WITH SPECTACULAR EXTRA DECORATION · BARBELL-SHAPED CAPPED COLUMNS · LONG SLENDER BITS OF ICE · LITTLE FROZEN PELLETS · FLAT-EDGED SIX-SIDED HEXAGONS

*Find
six different
kinds of snowflakes.*

On the seventh day of winter,
our chores are now complete.
Seven stacks of firewood
are piled up nice and neat.

ASH BRANCH DANGLES WINGED SEEDS · CHERRY TREE SPORTS REDDISH BARK · BASSWOOD BRANCH HOLDS SEED BALLS · ASPEN TREE GROWS SMOOTH GREENISH BARK · OAK TREE KEEPS DRIED LEAVES · BEECH TWIGS HAVE POINTY BUDS · BIRCH TREE HAS PEELING BARK

Identify
seven sorts of leafless trees,
dormant for the winter.

On the eighth day of winter,
o'er drifts both deep and tall,
we hike on eight broad snowshoes
and don't sink in at all.

SNOWSHOE HARE WITH HUGE HIND FEET · RUFFED GROUSE WITH BRISTLY TOES · RED SQUIRREL WITH LONG TOES · FISHER WITH BIG BLACK FEET · LYNX WITH LARGE HAIRY FEET · WHITE WEASEL WITH BIG FEET · DEER MOUSE WITH LONG TOES · WOLF SPIDER LIGHT AS SNOW

*Watch for
eight animals
staying on top of the snow.*

On the ninth day of winter,
we've stocked our icy fort
with nine big piles of snowballs –
there's no way we'll run short!

MOURNING CLOAK BUTTERFLIES HIBERNATE

BLOBS OF TENT-CATERPILLAR EGGS

LADYBUGS CLUSTER

STEM GALL HOLDS GOLDENROD FLY LARVA

QUEEN YELLOW-JACKET WASP HIBERNATES

LEAFY PROMETHEA MOTH COCOON HANGS

LUMPY LUNA MOTH COCOON HIDES

CARPENTER ANTS HIBERNATE

WOOLYBEAR CATERPILLAR HIDES

Discover
nine ways
insects wait out winter.

On the tenth day of winter,
marks on the pathway show
our mukluks, boots, and fur feet:
ten footprints in fresh snow.

Notice
ten trails
left by winter-active critters.

On the eleventh day of winter,
with truly awesome speed,
eleven evening grosbeaks
devour all our seed.

HEADFIRST RED-BREASTED NUTHATCH
CLINGING DOWNY WOODPECKER
FLYING HAIRY WOODPECKER
VELVETY GREY JAY
BROWN PINE SISKIN
HEADFIRST WHITE-BREASTED NUTHATCH
BLACK-AND-WHITE CHICKADEE
GREENISH BROWN GOLDFINCH
BRILLIANT BLUE JAY
SOOTY BACKED JUNCO
ROSEY PURPLE FINCH

Identify
eleven types of birds
that stay for the winter.

On the twelfth day of winter,
let's have a party here.
We'll bake twelve dozen cookies
to welcome the New Year!

FOX FOLLOWS A GROUSE · RED SQUIRREL EATS PINE SEEDS · OTTER DEVOURS A FISH · OWL CATCHES A MOUSE · PORCUPINE NIBBLES BARK · MARTEN EATS STARVED DEER · SPRUCE GROUSE EATS FIR NEEDLES · DEER MOUSE EATS SEEDS · SHREW EATS A SPIDER · WEASEL CATCHES A VOLE · CHICKADEE LOOKS FOR INSECTS · HARE NIBBLES BUDS

Search for
twelve hungry animals
finding something to eat.

What Happens on Winter Days?

Evergreen trees such as *balsam firs* are well adapted to cold an snow. Their needle-leaves have a waxy coating and sma surface areas; these features help evergreens conserve moistu during winter. The conical shape of a fir helps snow slide off limbs don't break from the weight of accumulated snow. Bu for next year's growth are tightly attached onto the branches.

balsam fir needles and buds

People aren't the only ones who like to slide on snow. *Otters* slide to travel over snow. When they go overland, they bound a few paces then slide for a stretch, bound a little, slide a bit. It must feel good, for in play they repeatedly use a single downhill slide. *Ravens* seem to glide just for fun. The first time a raven slides or rolls down a mound of snow or a snowy roof might be by accident. But then the bird will do it again and again, wings flapping and legs flailing.

raven's feather

After you make your own angel wings, look around for other telltale wi prints. A pair of large impressions at the end of some tiny tracks shows where owl dropped from above to catch a meal of mouse. Wing imprints and pelletli droppings show the tunnel from a *ruffed grouse's* nighttime snow burrow. Sm wing impressions in fresh snow are left by flocks of *pine siskins* as th forage for fallen birch seeds.

ruffed grouse droppings

minnows

The pond is frozen, but there's a lot of life down under the ice. During winter the water is warmest at the bottom, and aquatic critters carry on, safe from freezing. A *snapping turtle* waits out winter buried in the mud, its breathing and heartbeat greatly slowed. A *beaver* leaves her dark and cozy lodge to swim to her family's food cache of willow and aspen branches, submerged under the water. Hungry *bluegills* search for insect larvae or minnows and *dragonfly nymphs* prowl the pond bottom, looking for food.

Whether your thermometer reads in Fahrenheit or Celsius, twenty-five degrees below zero is cold! How do wild animals deal with cold? In an underground burrow, a *chipmunk* hibernates, rousing occasionally to nibble stored seeds. Sheltered by the snowpack, *voles* huddle together or travel along ground-level runways. A *wood frog,* buried under leaves and snow, is frozen stiff. In the spring, the frog will thaw and be able to move again.

kinglets

Feathers fluffed to trap insulating air, tiny *kinglets* hunt by day for frozen caterpillars and snuggle together at night, shivering to stay warm. *Garter snakes* hibernate deep below ground where the soil does not freeze.

The shape and size of snowflakes is determined by the temperature and humidity in the clouds where they begin to form. Little pellets of snow are *graupel;* these start as crystals and are coated with frozen droplets of moisture as they fall. *Plate crystals* are flat-edged hexagons (6-sided shapes). *Stellar crystals* are intricate 6-pointed stars. Spectacular *stellar hexagonal plate crystals* are created when cloud conditions change as the crystals are being formed. *Capped columns* can be tall and thin or short and stout. Much of what a

ellar crystal

storm deposits is *needle crystals:* long slender bits of ice frozen together.

peel of birch bark

In winter, trees that shed their leaves can look a lot alike. To figure out which bare tree is which, look for subtle clues. The bark of *birch* trees peels and curls. The winged seeds of *ash* trees hang in clusters. *Cherry* trees have dark reddish bark freckled with horizontal markings. Small seed balls beneath a wing-shaped leaf identify a *basswood*. *Aspens* have a light-colored, smooth bark with a greenish tinge. Dried brown leaves often stay attached to *oaks* all winter long. *Beech* trees have buds that are brownish, long, and pointed.

Snowshoes enable us to walk in deep snow by spreading our weight over a large area. Many critters navigate the snow in similar ways. A *snowshoe hare* is named for the huge hind feet that keep it from sinking in fluffy snow. During autumn, comblike projections grow on a *ruffed grouse's* toes so that during winter it has wide feet. Lightweights like *red squirrels* and *deer mice* have long toes that keep them from sinking. *Fishers* and *weasels* simply have big feet for their size. Stiff hairs on the bottoms of a *lynx's* big feet make those feet even bigger. A *wolf spider* is so light it stays on the snow's surface.

ruffed grouse

Protection is the name of the game for insects trying to make it through winter without being eaten. A leafy-looking *Promethea moth cocoon* hangs from a branch and a *Luna moth cocoon* rests among dry leaves. *Carpenter ants* hibernate in a gallery of tunnels deep within a dead log. *Woolybear caterpillars* hide under leaf litter, and sometimes freeze solid. *Mourning cloak butterflies* hibernate in hollow trees. Hardened foam shields *tent-caterpillar eggs* laid on a twig. Adult *ladybugs* cluster together. A *goldenrod fly larva* makes a plant's tissues create a protective growth, or gall, around it. A queen *yellow-jacket wasp* hangs cold within a shelter of leaves.

ladybugs

Right after a new snow is the perfect time to follow tracks. Huge doglike tracks: a *wolf*. Small prints, from bush to sapling: a *deer mouse*. Wide three-toed bird tracks: a *ruffed grouse*. Tree-to-tree: a *red squirrel*. A pair of large marks followed by two small ones: a bounding *hare*. Webbed prints and slide marks on the ice: an *otter*. Along the shoreline, paired prints go by a patch of open water: a *mink* searches for dinner. A trail of V-shaped marks: a wandering *deer*. Tiny prints with a tail mark: a busy *shrew*. Small doglike tracks: a *fox*.

wolf track

Winter birds find food on their own, but they always appreciate a handout. Sunflower seeds are favorites of *chickadees, purple finches,* and both *white-breasted* and *red-breasted nuthatches*. Add mixed small seeds to the feeder to bring in *goldfinches, juncos,* or *pine siskins*. Put out cracked corn and some peanuts – *blue jays* and *grey jays* will love it, and so will the squirrels. Hang a bag of suet for the *hairy* and *downy woodpeckers*. And keep an eye on your filled feeder after dark: if you're lucky you might see a *flying squirrel*.

ing squirrel

As the New Year begins, we celebrate with food and friends. Outside, animals hunt for food that is critical to their survival. A *deer mouse* nibbles seeds and dried berries, while a *shrew* chomps on a spider. A *weasel* plunges down a snow tunnel to catch a sleepy vole, while a *chickadee* searches for insects in a tree stump. A *hare* nibbles willow buds as a *red squirrel* peels pine cone scales to get the seeds. A hungry *fox* follows a grouse trail. On the ice, an *otter* devours a fish; nearby, a *great horned owl* catches a mouse. A *porcupine* eats inner bark from a towering hemlock as a *marten* feeds on a starved deer. And high in a balsam fir, a *spruce grouse* nibbles on green needles.

spruce grouse eating balsam fir needles

Earth's axis is an imaginary line that runs between the North and South Poles. Earth spins a full turn on this axis every twenty-four hours, giving us day and night. At the same time, Earth is traveling around the sun, completing one rotation each year.

Earth's axis is tilted at an angle, so as the earth orbits the sun, half of it is tipped toward the sun and half is tipped away. This tilt causes the seasons. When the North Pole is pointed away from the sun, we have winter in the Northern Hemisphere. The days are short, temperatures are cold, and often there is snow and ice.

Animals have ways to deal with winter's cold, hungry months. Some animals migrate. Ducks, geese, and many small birds fly south. Monarch butterflies flutter to warm locations. Herds of elk or deer move to sheltered areas. Other animals hibernate. Bears, raccoons, and skunks feast during summer and autumn and grow fat. During winter, they alternately sleep and wake up, but their bodies have changed so they cannot eat or eliminate. Chipmunks and woodchucks spend summer hoarding food underground. During winter, they have periods of wakefulness, when they eat and eliminate, and periods of torpor, when heart and breathing rates drop. Most reptiles and amphibians find sheltered places, where their bodies will not freeze, and endure a long, cold wait.

Many animals remain active during winter, working to find food and stay warm. Mammals put on thick coats; snowshoe hares and weasels even grow white winter coats for camouflage. Red squirrels plan ahead to save food; they collect cones in huge piles. Grey jays hide food on tree trunks and branches.

Winter may help some predators. Deep snow makes it hard for deer to escape large predators such as wolves. Weasels hunting voles in under-snow tunnels are protected from other predators. Dormant insects that aren't well hidden make easy meals for birds, shrews, or moles.

Amazingly, some animals have winter birthdays. When food supplies are ample, voles reproduce and raise young beneath the snow, and a tiny least weasel might have a litter of winter babies.